D1377642

F. Isabel Campoy

Alma Flor Ada

Celebrate
Chinese New Year
with the Fong Family

Illustrated by **Mima Castro**
Translated by **Joe Hayes** and **Sharon Franco**

ALFAGUARA

The Fong family and the Sanchez family are very good friends.

The Fongs have invited the Sanchez family to ring in the New Year with them. They'll be celebrating for many days!

2

The Sanchez family has heard a lot about Chinese New Year celebrations. They are all very excited, especially Nico. He loves to learn about new things, and he loves to take pictures of them.

"Watch out, Nico!" Sue shouts. "There's a bus behind you!"

3

"Dad told us we should bring you oranges and tangerines," Bea says.

"That means you are wishing us well," says Mrs. Fong. "These fruits stand for gold and happiness."

"What does this poster say?" asks Nico, as curious as ever.

"Good luck," Sue explains.

"Watch out, Nico!" shouts Ben. "You're going to fall!"

5

The Fong family and the Sanchez family walk around the market in Chinatown. There are so many colors and so many delicious smells!

"I love loquats and candied coconut," says Sue.

"Can we buy dates?" Bea asks.

"And red melon seeds!" Sue says.

"We already have all that at home. But we can always have more. I like to have a big tray for guests," says Mrs. Fong.

"Watch out, Nico!" Mom shouts. "Watch out for those firecrackers!"

Everyone gathers together for a very special dinner.
Mr. Fong lights incense and candles.

"Yummy! Everything looks so tasty. And I'm so
hungry!" says Nico.

"We can't start eating yet, Nico," Mr. Fong explains.
"Once the incense finishes burning, our ancestors
will have finished their dinner. Then we can eat."

The day of the parade arrives. It's the last day of the celebration. The street is full of people. There are bright colors everywhere and everyone is filled with joy.

"Here comes Gum Lung, the dragon!" Ben shouts excitedly. "It's really long!"

"There must be about a hundred men under that dragon!" says Mr. Fong.

"Where is Nico?" asks Sue.

"Look!" says Bea. "He's under the dragon."

"Nico, get out from under there," Dad says.

The parade moves on.

And Nico is lost again!

Everybody is looking for him— his mom,
his dad, his sister, and the Fongs.

Where can he be?

"Look, everybody!" Sue shouts. "Nico is on the float with the Queen of Chinatown!"

"He's taking pictures," Ben says.

"As usual," says Mr. Sanchez. "The dragon has one hundred legs and Nico will have one hundred photos."

What is Chinese New Year?

In the United States, the year begins on January 1st. However, not everybody celebrates New Year's Day on that date.

The Chinese culture, for example, has a different calendar. Chinese people celebrate their new year several weeks later. The first day of the Chinese year falls on a different date every year. It is usually in February, but sometimes it comes at the end of January.

The Chinese New Year is celebrated in China and Taiwan. Chinese people who live in other places all over the world also celebrate this holiday.

North America

United States

San Francisco

Los Angeles

New York

In the United States, large Chinese New Year celebrations take place in cities such as San Francisco, New York, and Los Angeles. Many Chinese-Americans who live there carry on the traditions of their culture.

The Chinese New Year celebration lasts for 15 days. The decorations, food, and activities all have a special meaning. Each thing means good wishes for the coming year.

In houses, streets, and temples, people hang paper lanterns and red signs with words written in Chinese. In the Chinese culture, red is the color of happiness.

People put out flowering plants, jars full of flowers, and trays with oranges, tangerines, and dried fruit in their homes. The flowers are for wealth and success. The oranges and tangerines stand for happiness. And the dried fruit can mean many things, such as health, unity, and joy.

The night before New Year's Day is called New Year's Eve. It is dedicated to the family. The whole family gathers for a big dinner. They also pray and remember their ancestors—or family members who have died.

For dinner they eat fish, seafood, chicken, dumplings, noodles, fruit, and sweet cakes. Long uncut noodles stand for long life. Fish means abundance. Chicken is for success.

After dinner, elders and children receive a special gift. They get red envelopes with money inside. At midnight, the streets and the sky light up with fireworks!

On the last day of the celebration, there is a big parade. The streets are filled with bright colors and the smell of firecrackers. There are bands playing music and there are also dancers. There is joy everywhere.

The lion and dragon dances are two of the most spectacular events in the parade. It is said that these animals chase away bad things and attract good ones.

Can you see the people under those costumes? You have to be very strong to carry those heavy heads!

Many other communities celebrate New Year's Day on a date other than January 1st. Jewish and Thai people are just two examples.

Jewish people celebrate their new year in September or October. This holiday is called *Rosh Hashanah*. They pray, throw pieces of bread into the water, and play a trumpet made from a ram's horn. They also eat apples dipped in honey, so that the new year will be "sweet."

In Thailand, the new year is celebrated in April with a festival called *Songkran*. Thai people throw buckets of water at each other because they want lots of rain to come. Rain is needed to grow crops.

If you like New Year's Day, now you know how to celebrate it several times throughout the year! Wherever you go, New Year's Day is always a holiday full of joy and good wishes.

Chinese New Year parade in Hong Kong.
© Kevin Fleming/CORBIS

Two girls at the Chinese New Year celebration in Paris, France.
© Prat Thierry/CORBIS SYGMA

Chinese New Year parade in Honolulu, Hawaii, U.S.A.
© Douglas Peebles/CORBIS

Chinese New Year celebration in New York City U.S.A.'s Chinatown neighborhood.
© Ramin Talaie/CORBIS

Chinese New Year celebration in Los Angeles, California, U.S.A.
© Nik Wheeler/CORBIS

A young girl and her grandmother celebrate Chinese New Year at home.
© Royalty-Free/CORBIS

Banners with New Year's greetings decorate a street in San Francisco's Chinatown neighborhood in California, U.S.A. during the Chinese New Year festivities.
© Morton Beebe/CORBIS

Poster with the Chinese symbol for happiness; a traditional Chinese New Year decoration.
© Royalty-Freee/CORBIS

On the eve of Chinese New Year, a man carries a kumquat tree home to bring prosperity. Victoria Park Market, Hong Kong.
© Kevin Fleming/CORBIS

Plants and flowers for sale in Victoria Park Market, in Hong Kong, during the Chinese New Year celebration.
© Kevin Fleming/CORBIS

A Chinese-American girl serves tea to her grandmother during a Chinese New Year dinner in San Francisco, California, U.S.A.
© Phil Schermeister/CORBIS

A Chinese-American family enjoys their New Year's dinner in San Francisco, California, U.S.A.
© Phil Schermeister/CORBIS

Traditional Chinese New Year dinner foods in a home in San Francisco, California, U.S.A.
© Phil Schermeister/CORBIS

A Chinese-American girl opens her Lai See, a traditional gift given to children and elders during the Chinese New Year celebration. San Francisco, California, U.S.A.
© Phil Schermeister/CORBIS

Fireworks.
© Paul Freytag/zefa/CORBIS

Artists in elaborate traditional dress participate in the Chinese New Year parade in Paris, France.
© J. L. Bulcao/CORBIS

Artists in elaborate traditional dress participate in the Chinese New Year parade in Paris, France.
© J. L. Bulcao/CORBIS

Show with drums and cymbals during the Chinese New Year celebration in Beijing, China.
© Karen Su/CORBIS

Dragon dance during the Chinese New Year parade in Singapore.
© Ted Streshinsky/CORBIS

Lion dance during the Chinese New Year celebration in the Chinatown neighborhood in Manila, Philippines.
© Paul A. Souders/CORBIS

Lion dance during the Chinese New Year parade in Hong Kong.
© Kevin Fleming/CORBIS

Orthodox Jews pray and blow the shofar during the Rosh Hashanah celebration in Jerusalem, Israel.
© Richard T. Nowitz/CORBIS

A group of Jews hold the Taschlich ceremony during the Rosh Hashanah celebration at Battery Park City, in New York City, U.S.A.
© Ramin Talaie/CORBIS

Dancers in traditional dress take part in a parade during the Songkran Festival in Chiangmai, Thailand.
© Kevin R. Morris/CORBIS

A group of young women throw buckets of water during the Songkran Festival in Chiangmai, Thailand.
© Kevin R. Morris/CORBIS

Celebrate and Grow

Throughout history, and in all parts of the world, people get together to celebrate historic anniversaries, commemorate an important person's life, or to ring in a special period of the year. Common to all these celebrations is the acknowledgment that life is a marvelous gift, and that getting together with family and friends makes us happy.

In a multicultural society, like that found in the United States, the fact that so many diverse groups live so closely together invites us to know our own culture better, and to discover the cultures of others. Anyone who explores his or her own culture recognizes his or her own identity in the mirror, and affirms his or her sense of belonging to a group. By learning about different cultures, we can observe life as it appears through the windows of those cultures.

This series offers children the opportunity to get close to the rich cultural landscape of our communities.

The Chinese New Year

Living in San Francisco gives us the opportunity to participate in Latino festivals in the Mission District, to taste Philippine, Hindu, Vietnamese, and African cuisine in many restaurants, and to enjoy the Chinese New Year in the heart of the city. The joy of this celebration fills many Chinese storefronts with the color red, and a walk down Grant Avenue practically turns into a party!

We would like to thank our friend Dr. Janice Young for having shared the knowledge of her traditions with us, and for her advice on the development of this book.

F. Isabel Campoy and Alma Flor Ada

To Julia Canals and to Violeta, with the promise of a get-together in San Francisco.
FIC

To Sophie Barr and to Adrián Lafuente, the newest shoots on our lush family tree.
AFA

© This edition:
2006, Santillana USA Publishing Company, Inc.
2105 NW 86th Avenue
Miami, FL 33122
www.santillanausa.com

Text © 2006 Alma Flor Ada and F. Isabel Campoy

Managing Editor: Isabel C. Mendoza
Copyeditor: Eileen Robinson
Art Director: Mónica Candelas
Production: Cristina Hiraldo

Alfaguara is part of the **Santillana Group**, with offices in the following countries:
ARGENTINA, BOLIVIA, CHILE, COLOMBIA, COSTA RICA, DOMINICAN REPUBLIC, ECUADOR,
EL SALVADOR, GUATEMALA, MEXICO, PANAMA, PARAGUAY, PERU, PUERTO RICO, SPAIN,
UNITED STATES, URUGUAY, AND VENEZUELA

Celebrate Chinese New Year with the Fong Family
ISBN 10: 1-59820-126-3
ISBN 13: 978-1-59820-126-0

Published in the United States of America.
Printed in Colombia by D'vinni S.A.

12 11 10 09 08 07   2 3 4 5 6 7

Library of Congress Cataloging-in-Publication Data

Campoy, F. Isabel.
   [Celebra el ano nuevo chino con la familia Fong. English]
   Celebrate Chinese New Year with the Fong family / by F. Isabel
Campoy and Alma Flor Ada ; illustrated by Mima Castro.
    p. cm. — (Stories to celebrate)
   Summary: The Sanchez and the Fong families get together to
celebrate Chinese New Year. Includes facts about the holiday.
   ISBN 1-59820-126-3
   [1. Chinese New Year—Fiction. 2. Chinese Americans—Fiction.
3. Hispanic Americans—Fiction.]
   I. Ada, Alma Flor. II. Castro, Mima, ill. III. Title. IV. Series.

PZ7.C16153Ce 2006
[E]—dc22   2006025502